The Gift of the
Little People

About the Six Seasons of the Asiniskaw Īthiniwak Series

This series is about the Asiniskaw Īthiniwak (Rocky Cree) of Northern Manitoba. Corresponding to the six seasons of sīkwan (spring), nīpin (summer), takwakin (fall), mikiskow (freeze-up), pipon (winter), and mithoskamin (break-up), the books explore the language, culture, knowledge, territory, and history of the 17th-century Rocky Cree people through story and images. The groundbreaking series centres Indigenous ways of knowing and includes insights from a wide range of disciplines—cross-cultural education, history, archaeology, anthropology, linguistics, literature, oral culture and storytelling, experiential and community-based learning, and art.

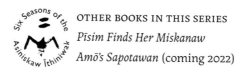

**A Six Seasons of the
Asiniskaw Īthiniwak Story**

The Gift of the Little People

Story by William Dumas
Illustrated by Rhian Brynjolson

Canada Council   Conseil des arts
for the Arts   du Canada

We acknowledge the support of the Canada Council for the Arts.
Nous remercions le Conseil des arts du Canada de son soutien.

HighWater Press gratefully acknowledges the financial support of
the Province of Manitoba through the Department of Sport, Culture and Heritage
and the Manitoba Book Publishing Tax Credit, and the Government of Canada
through the Canada Book Fund (CBF), for our publishing activities.

HighWater Press is an imprint of Portage & Main Press.
Printed in Canada by Friesens
Design by Jennifer Lum

Additional Contributions
Storywork: Warren Cariou
Transcription and Text Editing: Melanie Braith, Michael Minor
Consultation: Margaret Dumas

Library and Archives Canada Cataloguing in Publication
Title: The gift of the Little People / story by William Dumas ; illustrated by Rhian Brynjolson.
Names: Dumas, William, 1949- author. | Brynjolson, Rhian, illustrator.
Description: Series statement: A six seasons of the Asiniskaw Īthiniwak story
Some words in Rocky Cree dialect.
Identifiers: Canadiana (print) 20210245441 Canadiana (ebook) 20210245549
ISBN 9781553799924 (hardcover) | ISBN 9781553799931 (EPUB) | ISBN 9781553799948 (PDF)
Subjects: LCSH: Indigenous peoples—Hudson Bay Region—History—Juvenile fiction.
LCGFT: Picture books. Classification: LCC PS8607.U44318 G54 2022 | DDC jc813/.6—dc23

25 24 23 22   1 2 3 4 5

FSC
www.fsc.org
MIX
Paper from
responsible sources
FSC® C016245

ENVIRONMENTAL BENEFITS STATEMENT
Portage & Main Press saved the following resources
by printing the pages of this book on chlorine free
paper made with 10% post-consumer waste.

TREES	WATER	SOLID WASTE	GREENHOUSE GASES
1 FULLY GROWN	300 GALLONS	5 POUNDS	580 POUNDS

Environmental impact estimates were made using the Environmental Paper Network
Paper Calculator 4.0. For more information visit www.papercalculator.org

HIGHWATER
PRESS
www.highwaterpress.com
Winnipeg, Manitoba
Treaty 1 Territory and homeland of the Métis Nation

Dedicated to my father, Jacob Dumas.
My father was a second-generation trapline holder,
fisherman, and storyteller from Nelson House.
His Rocky Cree stories live on today in many forms,
including this book.

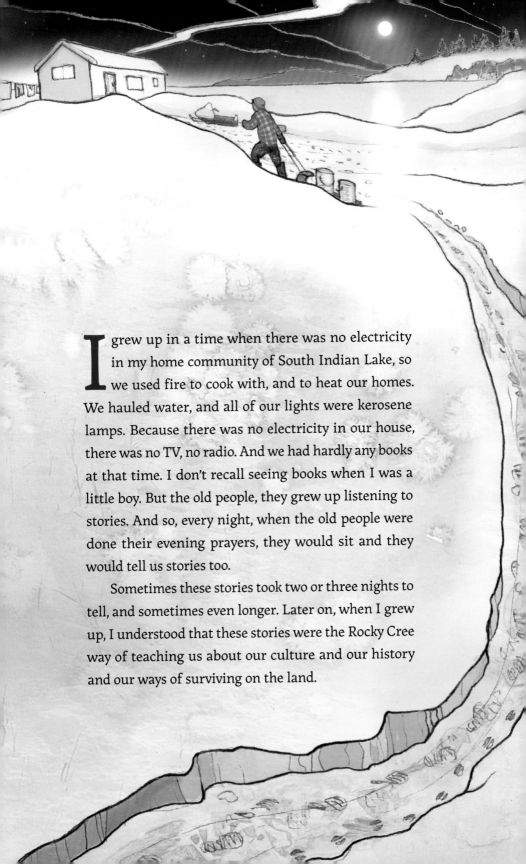

I grew up in a time when there was no electricity
in my home community of South Indian Lake, so
we used fire to cook with, and to heat our homes.
We hauled water, and all of our lights were kerosene
lamps. Because there was no electricity in our house,
there was no TV, no radio. And we had hardly any books
at that time. I don't recall seeing books when I was a
little boy. But the old people, they grew up listening to
stories. And so, every night, when the old people were
done their evening prayers, they would sit and they
would tell us stories too.

Sometimes these stories took two or three nights to
tell, and sometimes even longer. Later on, when I grew
up, I understood that these stories were the Rocky Cree
way of teaching us about our culture and our history
and our ways of surviving on the land.

"Kayās nōsisimak, kayās, kimithwasin askiy, kipiyatakan. Kimithwayāniwan."

One group of characters that the Elders always told stories about was the Little People. The Little People are no taller than your knee, and I think you could compare them to the leprechauns—except they don't have pointed ears. There are three different kinds of Little People. First there are the ones known as mīmīkwīsiwak, which means "static-voiced people." They are called that because their voices sound like the static you hear when an old radio is stuck between two stations. The second kind of Little People look a bit like trolls: short and stout. The third kind of Little People look exactly like us, mirror images of the people that live in our world— even you and me. They are medicine people, mappers, hunters, trappers, canoe builders...they all have their specific skills, just like us.

I had a special curiosity about the Little People ever since I was a kid, partly because of the stories the Elders told, but also because many of our friends and relatives said they had actually seen the Little People at one time or another. My father was an amazing storyteller, so one night I gave him tobacco and I said, "Dad, tell me a story about the Little People." I was getting older by then, but he lay down beside me on the bed, just like I was a little boy, and he started telling a story.

Kākakiw

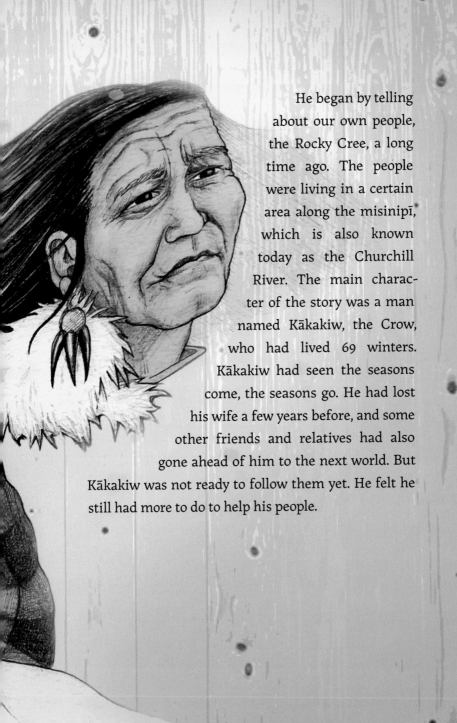

He began by telling about our own people, the Rocky Cree, a long time ago. The people were living in a certain area along the misinipī, which is also known today as the Churchill River. The main character of the story was a man named Kākakiw, the Crow, who had lived 69 winters. Kākakiw had seen the seasons come, the seasons go. He had lost his wife a few years before, and some other friends and relatives had also gone ahead of him to the next world. But Kākakiw was not ready to follow them yet. He felt he still had more to do to help his people.

One morning Kākakiw woke up to the sound of the birds saying their morning prayers, beginning the mantra of their daily life. He thought about the excitement people had felt during the past winter. The previous fall there had been reports of a new people that had come into the big bay, mistiwāsahak, that we also know as Hudson Bay—a new people who had come in big boats. These people had brought amazing tools that the Rocky Cree had never seen. They had these pots made out of a special material that would cook food faster than any of the pots the Rocky Cree had. And they had beautiful cups that wouldn't break if you dropped them. They had axes that could cut trees faster than their stone axes, knives that were really sharp, and beautiful cloth, different from the moose hides and caribou hides that the Rocky Cree used.

And the people said, "Boy, this is exciting. And all they want in exchange for these special things are the furs that are so plentiful here: beaver and mink, marten, lynx, fox." That's what these new visitors wanted. You give them some furs and they would give you these things.

Come springtime, when the misinipī opened, they decided to send a delegation out to the big bay to trade. The ones that were chosen to go were younger people, probably in their mid-twenties. And the leader of that group, his wife came along because she was a strong paddler and a really good worker out on the land when they travelled. So they gathered all the furs they had and loaded them up into the canoes. And away they went. They left, gone. And Kākakiw just carried on with his daily activities at home. He had an apprentice, a young medicine woman, that he taught how to make medicines, because everyone with valuable knowledge had to have an ongoing apprentice. And he also had a young man who looked after him, his ōskātis. So, their little village worked like a machine, even when the group of paddlers was not there. Everybody had their responsibilities, everybody did their part.

It's a long way from misinipī to the big bay, mistiwāsahak. Today it might take someone most of the summer to paddle all the way to the bay and back, loaded down with furs and trade goods. But back then, because the people were so healthy, it took only a few days to make that journey. So it was not long before Kākakiw heard the cries of happiness down by the water when the kids first noticed the canoes coming back home. Everyone rushed down to greet the paddlers, eager to see what kind of things they had traded for, interested to learn about these new people who had come in their big boats. It turned out the stories were true: when they unloaded the canoes, there were shiny pots and cups, very sharp knives, axes, and rolls of beautiful bright-coloured cloth.

The people had a feast that night to celebrate their good luck in making these trades. There was drumming and dancing, and the paddlers were asked again and again to tell everyone about these strange visitors from far away who were so fond of furs. Everyone was happy and they looked forward to making more trades with these visitors in the future.

But one evening a couple of days later, just as it was getting dark, the people heard someone crying for help down at the lake. They ran down there and saw that it was the young woman who had gone with the paddlers to the bay. Her husband lay at the bottom of the canoe, and he was sweating.

"What happened?" everyone asked. They were in a bad panic. None of them had ever seen anything like this.

"I don't know," she said. "We were going about harvesting, hunting, and all of a sudden he just dropped. He started sweating like he is now. Soon he became delirious, and I couldn't understand what he was trying to tell me."

They carried the young man up to the village. That night old Kākakiw worked on him, and the young medicine woman helped too, singing songs, praying, giving him medicine. But by dawn the young man passed into the spirit world. He was gone. Then, only a few hours later, another of the men who had gone to trade fell suddenly ill. He didn't last. Soon the young woman whose husband had died fell ill too.

That's how it started. Many people were getting sick. Day and night, old Kākakiw and the young medicine woman and the ōskātis, they looked after the people, trying to keep them alive, constantly praying, going from tent to tent, feeding them, giving them medicine, giving them care. But the people, slowly they were going. And eventually, after a few nights, old Kākakiw went into his tent. He couldn't take it anymore. He was tired physically, emotionally, spiritually. He was at a loss because he didn't know what was going on. He didn't know what was happening to the people and he was so tired from lack of sleep. So was the young medicine woman, and he had told her to go home and try to sleep. But no matter how tired he was, old Kākakiw never forgot to pray. He took his pipe out and he prayed and he asked for help:

"We're at a loss, there is nothing we can do. We keep losing person after person. You know we're a small band. There won't be many of us left in the next few days. We're not going to survive this. Please send us some help. We can no longer keep this up. We're at the end here."

kakisamowin

And he stoked his fire and went to sleep.

Sometime in the night, he heard somebody open-ing his tent flap, and he sat up and looked. At first he saw nothing. But then he looked down, and he saw this little man walking toward him…walking into his teepee. And the little man stopped there for a while, watching the fire, which was just about dead. Eventually the little guy walked up to the fire, picked up a couple of logs, and stoked the fire until it started burning again. Then he sat down on the ground and looked into the fire again.

"What do you want?" Kākakiw said.

"You sent for me."

"I asked for help, yes, but…"

"Yes, they sent me."

"But you're so small."

The little man said, "We're small, but we have the medicine that you need. We have it."

"Where is it?" Kākakiw asked.

"You know across the lake here, there is that high rock face? We're on the other side. You'll have to come through there to get it."

"But how am I going to do that?" He knew the place. It was a cliff of solid bedrock.

"With a canoe, of course!" the little man said. "You're going to paddle through it."

Kākakiw looked at the little man for a while. "You know what," he said. "This could be a very embarrassing situation. If I hit that rock with my little birchbark canoe, it's going to just blow up."

And the little man said, "What choice do you have?"

"Okay, when do we go for this medicine then?"

"Tomorrow. You go and wait a little ways from the rock face. Smoke your pipe. When the sun sets and it's gone, that's when the door opens. Paddle hard toward that rock face. Bring your ōskātis to help you."

"Okay…see you tomorrow night."

The little man got up, stoked the fire one more time for the old man, and left.

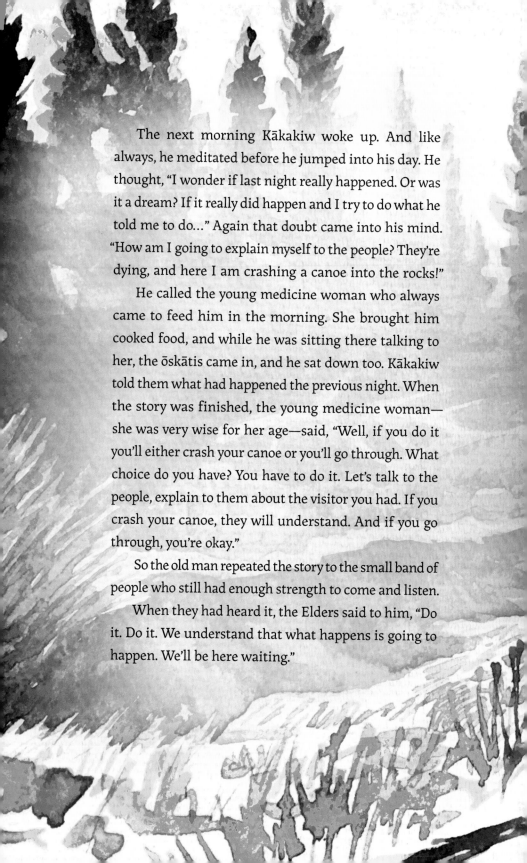

The next morning Kākakiw woke up. And like always, he meditated before he jumped into his day. He thought, "I wonder if last night really happened. Or was it a dream? If it really did happen and I try to do what he told me to do..." Again that doubt came into his mind. "How am I going to explain myself to the people? They're dying, and here I am crashing a canoe into the rocks!"

He called the young medicine woman who always came to feed him in the morning. She brought him cooked food, and while he was sitting there talking to her, the ōskātis came in, and he sat down too. Kākakiw told them what had happened the previous night. When the story was finished, the young medicine woman—she was very wise for her age—said, "Well, if you do it you'll either crash your canoe or you'll go through. What choice do you have? You have to do it. Let's talk to the people, explain to them about the visitor you had. If you crash your canoe, they will understand. And if you go through, you're okay."

So the old man repeated the story to the small band of people who still had enough strength to come and listen.

When they had heard it, the Elders said to him, "Do it. Do it. We understand that what happens is going to happen. We'll be here waiting."

So that day he told his ōskātis, "We're going to do it.
We have no choice."

Sure enough, by that evening they were sitting in
front of the steep rock face that the little man had told
him about. Kākakiw smoked his pipe as the sun was
going down. He smoked his pipe and prayed.

And when he was finished smoking his pipe he said,
"Nōsisim, paddle hard. I'll paddle hard too. When
we hit that rock, what happens is going to happen.
We have to go."

That young ōskātis believed in the old man
and he said, "Let's do it."
So they paddled really hard toward that rock
face, and as they hit the wall of solid rock—
their canoe went into it very smoothly.
It went right through the rock.

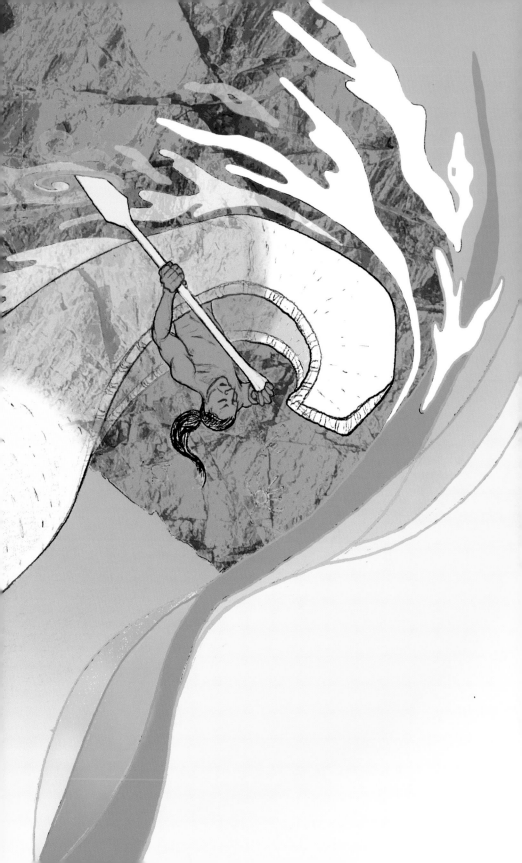

When they got to the other side, Kākakiw looked around. In front of him was like a mirror image. He saw a fire in the distance before them, and then he turned around and saw another identical fire behind them. It was the one in their village where the people were waiting for him to bring back the medicine.

"Well, I guess that's where we're supposed to go," he said, "toward the mirror image of our fire."

So they paddled slowly toward it, and as they got closer they saw a group of tiny children playing on the shore. When the children saw this giant boat coming toward them, they ran up the hill. They were scared. They ran up to the village and they were yelling about this monster boat coming toward them. The adult Little People, they came down to meet their visitors, their *big* visitors.

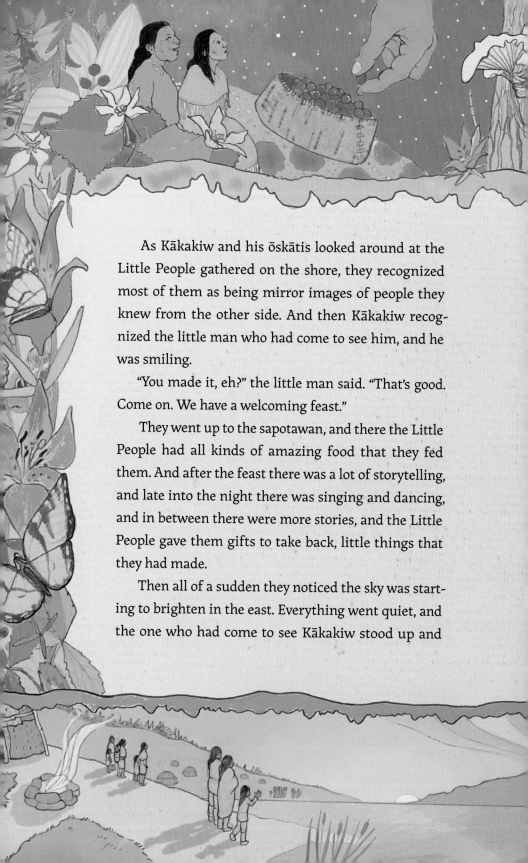

As Kākakiw and his ōskātis looked around at the Little People gathered on the shore, they recognized most of them as being mirror images of people they knew from the other side. And then Kākakiw recognized the little man who had come to see him, and he was smiling.

"You made it, eh?" the little man said. "That's good. Come on. We have a welcoming feast."

They went up to the sapotawan, and there the Little People had all kinds of amazing food that they fed them. And after the feast there was a lot of storytelling, and late into the night there was singing and dancing, and in between there were more stories, and the Little People gave them gifts to take back, little things that they had made.

Then all of a sudden they noticed the sky was starting to brighten in the east. Everything went quiet, and the one who had come to see Kākakiw stood up and

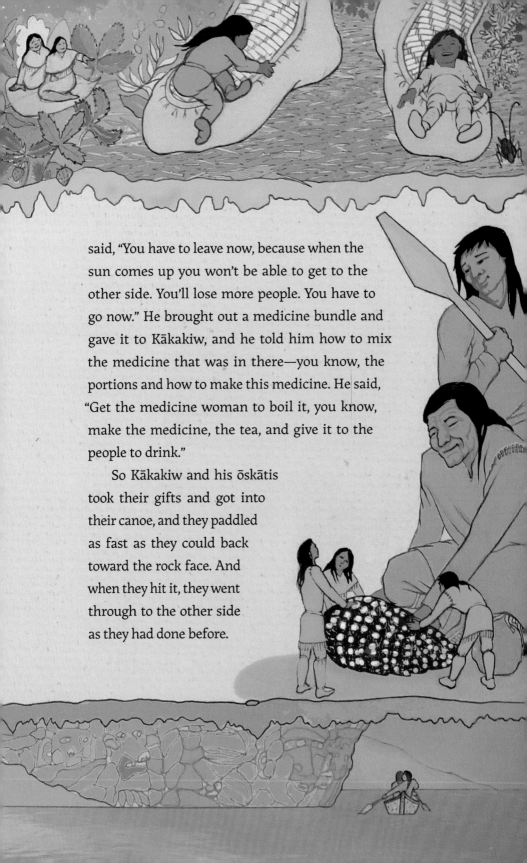

said, "You have to leave now, because when the sun comes up you won't be able to get to the other side. You'll lose more people. You have to go now." He brought out a medicine bundle and gave it to Kākakiw, and he told him how to mix the medicine that was in there—you know, the portions and how to make this medicine. He said, "Get the medicine woman to boil it, you know, make the medicine, the tea, and give it to the people to drink."

So Kākakiw and his ōskātis took their gifts and got into their canoe, and they paddled as fast as they could back toward the rock face. And when they hit it, they went through to the other side as they had done before.

Soon they arrived at the village, and they saw the young medicine woman waiting there. They gave her the medicine and she began to prepare it. A few days later, most of the people's health was restored.

They started moving around again, being healthy. And to this day, the Rocky Cree people use those medicines that were given by the Little People. We had lost a lot of relatives, but those medicines have helped keep our people alive ever since that time. And that's the story of how the Little People gave the Rocky Cree the medicine that we still use to cure sicknesses today.

The End.

Glossary

The Rocky Cree people—Asiniskaw Īthiniwak—speak the "TH" dialect of the Cree language. Each word of the Asiniskaw Īthiniwak language is connected to the land and contains the teachings of the ancestors. Rocky Cree territory is along the misinipī, also known as the Churchill River, which flows from Churchill Lake into Hudson Bay.

Asiniskaw Īthiniwak *(uh-seh-neh-scow* EE-*thi-neh-wuk)* Rocky People. This is what the Rocky Cree people call themselves in their language.

Kākakiw *(*KAH-*kah-kyu)* Crow. This word's meaning is related to the fact that it sounds like the call of a crow.

kakīsamowin *(kah-kee-*SAM-*o-win)* A traditional word for "prayer."

Kayās nōsisimak, kayās, kimithwasin askīy kipiyatakan. Kimithwayāniwan. *(ka-YASS no-SIS-ee-mak, ka-YASS, kee-MEETH-wa-sin as-KEE kip-ee-YA-ta-kan kee-MEETH-way-AN-ee-wan)* "A long time ago, my grandchildren—the earth was beautiful then. It was peaceful, and the people were well." This is a common way to start a story in the Rocky Cree tradition.

mīmīkwīsiwak *(mee-mee-KWE-see-wuk)* The static-voiced people. "Mī-mī-kwī" refers to the murmuring sound of their speech, which is something like the static of a radio between stations. Mīmīkwīsiwak are one of the three kinds of Little People—but not the ones that are the focus of this story.

misinipī *(meh-seh-NIH-pee)* Big water. "Misi" means big, and "nipī" means water. This word describes the Churchill River, which runs from the foothills of the Rocky Mountains to its end point at Hudson Bay.

mistiwāsahak *(MISS-ti-WASS-a-hak)* The big bay. From "misti" (big) and "wāsahak" (bay). This refers to Hudson Bay.

nōsisim *(NOH-sey-sim)* Grandchild. It means "one who is coming behind you" or "one whom you have a responsibility to teach holistically." In Rocky Cree teachings, "nōsisim" does not necessarily mean a blood relation, but rather refers to a relationship of protection and teaching.

ōskātis *(os-KAH-teece)* A young person, usually a teenager or younger, who is apprenticed to help and to learn from an older person. You are useful to your community when you are an ōskātis.

sapotawan *(SAH-POH-ta-wahn)* A structure built for larger gatherings, especially for ceremonies. It comes from "sapo," which means "to go through," referring to the entrance of the structure. The word also refers to specific ceremonies that occur within the sapotawan, such as the one described in the book *Amō's Sapotawan*.

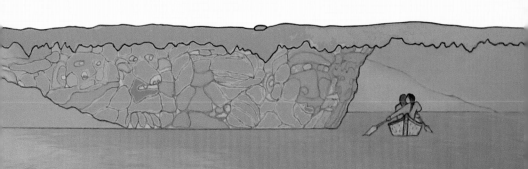

 **WILLIAM DUMAS**, a Rocky Cree storyteller, was born in South Indian Lake, Manitoba. For 25 years, he has been an educator and administrator; his passion for the Cree language and culture are well aligned with his current position as Cree Language and Culture Coordinator for the Nisichawayasihk (Nelson House) Education Authority. As the author of The Six Seasons of the Asiniskaw Īthiniwak series, William knows first-hand the power storytelling has to teach Indigenous youth where they come from and where they are going.

RHIAN BRYNJOLSON (she/her/hers) is a visual artist, author, book illustrator, and art educator. Rhian was named the Canadian Art Teacher of the Year in 2014. She is the author of *Teaching Art: A Complete Guide for the Classroom* and has illustrated 15 books for children. Rhian has worked with the River on the Run artist collective, making and performing art to raise awareness of environmental concerns affecting the Lake Winnipeg watershed. Rhian lives and works on the edge of Treaty 3 territory, in the boreal forest of eastern Manitoba. Her work is currently exhibited as part of the Virtual Water Gallery at www.virtualwatergallery.ca and at www.rhianbrynjolson.com.